BLENDED WHISKEY

AN AGENTS IRISH AND WHISKEY SHORT STORY

LAYLA REYNE

Blended Whiskey

Copyright © 2018, 2023 by Layla Reyne

All rights reserved. No part of this book may be reproduced or transmitted in any form or by any means, electronic or mechanical, including photocopying, recording, or by any information storage and retrieval system without the written permission of the copyright owner, and where permitted by law. Reviewers may quote brief passages in a review.

Cover Design: Cate Ashwood Designs

1Ed Editing: Deborah Nemeth, Julia Ganis

2Ed Editing: Adam Mongaya

Second Edition

August 2023

E-Book ISBN: 978-1-962010-08-5

Paperback ISBN: 978-1-962010-09-2

This is a work of fiction. Names, characters, places, and incidents are either the product of the author's imagination or are used fictitiously. Any resemblance to actual persons living or dead, business establishments, events, or locales is entirely coincidental. All person(s) depicted on the cover are model(s) used for illustrative purposes only. The author acknowledges the copyrights and trademarked status and trademark owners of any trademarks and copyrights mentioned in this work of fiction.

Content Warnings: Explicit sex; explicit language.

AUTHOR'S NOTE

This story takes place after the events of the original *Agents Irish and Whiskey* trilogy and *Tequila Sunrise* and will best be enjoyed as a continuation of the Whiskey Verse established therein rather than as a standalone. The events of Nic and Cam's trilogy, *Trouble Brewing,* follow from here.

YOU'RE INVITED

Aidan "Irish" Talley
and
Jameson "Whiskey" Walker
together with their family and friends
request the honor of your presence
at their wedding
Saturday, the Seventeenth of March
Two Thousand and Eighteen
at High Noon
Half Moon Bay, California

For all the Agents Irish and Whiskey fans

DANNY

Irish, Southern—same stock.

Danny had heard Jamie say that line, or some version of it, to Aidan numerous times over the past year and a half, but he'd never really understood it. Until today.

Standing at the top of the beach house stairs, watching as the Talley and Walker families mingled on the stone patio below, he finally got it. Jamie's Southern family had effortlessly meshed with their Irish one. Jamie's twin nieces had locked arms with Katie, the three of them in the middle of the redheaded tornado of Talley grandchildren. Jamie's sister had slid right in with Danny and Aidan's three siblings, and their mothers were already thick as thieves, plotting who knew what as they sipped champagne on the lounge chairs. Happiest of all was their father, who had added Jamie's brother-in-law, plus Jamie's best friend, Cam, to their woefully outnumbered ranks.

The beach house was also perfect for this casual rehearsal dinner and first meeting of the families. Maybe it was a little small for such a gathering, but the view from high atop a Half Moon Bay cliff rivaled that of the Ritz-Carlton up the road, where the wedding would be held tomorrow. The kitchen was also big and well-equipped enough for Jamie to work his magic, cooking up a dizzying array of Southern favorites: pulled pork, fried chicken, fried okra, skillet corn bread, and gallons of sweet tea, spiked with whiskey for the adults. All in all, the location, food, and company were perfect for the no-ties-allowed celebration. There would be more than enough formal wear tomorrow.

Danny tore his gaze from the stunning sunset and scanned the crowd for his better half. Finding her face missing, he glanced over his shoulder to the kitchen, then laughed at himself for thinking his wife would be there. To her credit, Mel was improving, but her skills with a knife were put to far better use running security for the family company or chasing down bounties.

"Here," came her smooth, commanding voice from the adjacent room. Mel sashayed over on high-heeled boots, glass of Bollinger in one hand, phone in the other. "Stylist called. He's at the hotel."

Danny set his Mason jar of spiked iced tea on the wide stair railing and draped his arm across her sweatered shoulders, the March night cool out here on the coast. "Time to kidnap a groom, then."

Another perk of this house—it would keep Aidan and Jamie apart the night before their wedding. Cam would stay here with the Walkers and Jamie, making sure that the groom didn't escape, while Mel and Danny secured Aidan at the Ritz with the rest of the Talleys.

Placing her glass next to his, Mel leaned against Danny's side and looped an arm around his waist. "Give 'em a few more minutes," she said. "I haven't seen either of them this relaxed in months."

Danny snickered against her temple, pressing a kiss there before he followed her gaze to the two grooms in the crowd below. Mel was right. He couldn't remember a time since the death of Aidan's first husband when his brother had looked this relaxed and happy. Propped against Jamie, one hand in his fiancé's back jeans pocket, Aidan drank from a bottle of beer and chatted animatedly with Jamie and their guests, probably about basketball.

"Everyone's having a good time," Mel said, a wistful smile in her voice.

"Any regrets we didn't do the same?"

They'd eloped last fall, their secret revealed after a near catastrophe at Christmas. It was a weight off their shoulders for everyone to know and for them to move in together, finally. Most of all, it was a relief that their worry of overshadowing Aidan and Jamie's big day hadn't come to pass.

"Fuck no." She turned her face up to him, smile sly, and Danny stole a quick kiss. "And besides, you'll be in a wedding tomorrow."

"So will you," he said with a wink.

"You ready?"

"To make sure the rings are tied to Katie's pillow and stand next to my big bro as he promises himself to Jamie?" He shrugged his free shoulder. "I got the easy job. How about you?"

Her gaze drifted out over the crowd, landing on Aidan

and Jamie again. "My script's not that hard to follow either, especially since Katie wrote their vows."

"That's not the only thing I meant." He reined in his smile and squeezed her shoulder. "Aidan was married to your brother, chica. I can't imagine this is easy."

"It's not," she admitted quietly, trying and failing to hide the melancholy he'd glimpsed in her dark eyes. "But they had a good ten years together before Gabe died. I hope Aidan gets many more years with Jamie."

Danny lowered his arm and curled it around her back, pulling her closer. "I heard there's a tribute to Gabe."

She nodded against his shoulder. "Arroz con leche for dessert. It was Jamie's idea. Aidan apparently makes it for him quite often."

Mel swung her other arm up around his middle, hugging him back, and they shared a moment of silence for their loved one lost.

"You know," Danny said after another couple of minutes, "there's something I've been meaning to ask you."

She leaned back in the circle of his arms. "What's that?

"Did you plan this?" He gestured at the merriment around them, then directly at Aidan and Jamie. "When you partnered the two of them?" They'd all wondered how that would go—a freshly-returned-to-work Aidan mentoring younger Cyber agent Jameson "Whiskey" Walker. No one could have predicted this, except maybe Danny's wife.

"I knew Jamie would be good for him," she said with a smirk. "But *this* exceeded my expectations."

"Well, in that case . . ." He retrieved their glasses, handed the flute to Mel, and tipped his Mason jar in her direction. "Job well done, wife."

"Thank you, husband." She clinked her glass against his. "This is one job I'll happily take credit for."

"We've got one more tonight," he added before swallowing the rest of the super sweet tea down. "You up for it?"

She finished her own glass of bubbly, then slid an arm through his. "Lead the way."

CAM

Cam tiptoed up the beach house's spiral staircase, lighting his way with the screen of his phone. Jamie's nieces had demanded a bedtime story from "Uncle Cam," and since he saw them so seldom, he wasn't about to refuse. He'd stuck his head and shoulders inside their pillow fort and woven a story about two rival dinosaurs who had become the best of friends after the Tyrannosaurus rex accidentally ripped off the triceratops's horn. A *Jurassic Park* version of his and Jamie's meeting and friendship, the former basketball star having injured Cam in a game his junior year of college. They'd been best friends ever since.

Cam was searching for his best friend now, on the main level of the house, when his phone screen brightened. He flipped it over and read the text from tonight's missing guest.

How'd the party go? Nic asked. **Everything good with the house?**

A work emergency had kept the Assistant US Attorney in San Francisco. Cam didn't doubt that—Nic was as much a workaholic as any of them—but he also wondered if the prosecutor's absence had more to do with some misguided sense of keeping the peace. Nic had dated Aidan what felt like eons ago, and despite moving past that, despite helping to save Katie last spring and the Talleys at Christmas, Nic still held himself back from Cam and their friends.

Good time. The house and the beer were perfect, Cam texted back. The beer at tonight's festivities had been from the brewery Nic co-owned; the house belonged to his business partner. **Everything good with work?**

Busy. Caught a major break in the case Aidan and I are working.

The heist one?

Aidan, now Special Agent in Charge of the FBI's San Francisco field office, had kept Cam, Assistant Special Agent in Charge, in the loop on the heist case. Cam had also heard Aidan utter more than a few frustrated Gaelic curses over it. This bit of news, if Aidan hadn't heard it already, would make a spectacular wedding present.

We'll need to bring you up to speed before he leaves. Aidan and Jamie were headed to Dublin for their honeymoon once Jamie wrapped up his coaching duties for the season.

Cam glanced out the bay window, spotting Jamie on the patio below. **Fill me in tomorrow?**

If I can make it.

And there went Nic, withdrawing again.

Not so fast, if Cam had anything to say about it. He wasn't putting on a tux only for his best friend's benefit. He'd wanted something from Nic for a while now—smart or not—and he was counting on the tux to help him get it.

Dominic . . . he texted.

Nic's one-word reply came right back. **Boston . . .**

Cam let him stew as he pulled two beers out of the fridge, hoping Nic would reach the answer he wanted.

The prosecutor got most of the way there. **I'll do my best to make it.**

One more little push . . . **Might be the only chance you get to see me in a monkey suit.**

Oh, well, when you put it that way, I'll be there with fucking bells on.

Cam grinned in the dark. **Promise?**

Goodnight, Boston.

Picking up the bottles—Gravity Imperial Stout, Cam's favorite from Nic's brewery—he started for the back door, typing as he walked. **Don't forget the beer.**

It's already at the hotel.

He searched his phone for the most obnoxious BoSox-Win GIF he could find and hit Send. Nic's icy blues would probably roll right out of his head.

Not expecting a response, Cam pocketed the phone and headed outside, down the stairs to the patio. Jamie sat straddling one of the picnic benches, bouncing a St. Mary's stress ball between his legs and staring at the Ritz up the beach, the hotel glowing like a haunted Scottish castle on its fog-shrouded cliff.

"Despite popular opinion," Cam said, "Talley is not a leprechaun. He won't magically appear, no matter how hard you wish it so."

Smiling, Jamie hauled his other leg over the bench, righting himself to face Cam across the table. "It's been a while since we've spent a night apart."

"Right before Christmas?"

Jamie nodded, rolling the ball under his palm.

Cam slid a bottle across the table to him. "Special occasion," he said, since Jamie didn't drink often.

"That it is." Jamie tipped the bottle back and took a long swallow, humming in approval. "It's good."

"Nic makes a good brew." Cam rotated the bottle between his hands, admiring the artistic label with the brewery's falling apricot logo. Nic had a whole other second job in addition to his important first one. He had his shit together, for real, whereas Cam's life and shit felt more scattered than ever.

"Where was he tonight?" Jamie asked, cutting off Cam's spiraling thoughts.

"What am I, his keeper?"

Jamie held up a hand. "You're the one who arranged this house with him."

Cam lowered his hackles. "His idea, actually, when I said you should have a proper wedding eve apart from your future husband."

An attractive blush streaked across Jamie's cheeks, his lips turned up in a shy smile, like he still couldn't believe what was about to happen. "I'll thank him tomorrow. He'll be at the wedding?"

"Said he'd do his best to make it. There was a break in one of his and Aidan's cases."

"Ah," Jamie said. "That explains the call Aidan stepped away for. He came back smiling like he'd won the lottery."

"Dammit," Cam cursed. "Thought I'd finally found a wedding present. I mean, what the fuck else can I get you two that you don't already have?"

"Hey," Jamie said, voice dropping into his coaching-moment register. "You left Boston and moved out here for us. I couldn't have left the Bureau, voluntarily or otherwise, and taken my dream job coaching basketball if I didn't know you were here to have Aidan's back. That's all the gift you needed to give us."

Cam hoped the sheen in his eyes wasn't visible in the dark. As it was, he had to take a long swallow of beer to force the lump down his throat. A comfortable silence settled as they nursed their beers to the sound of crashing waves, Jamie's gaze repeatedly straying up the beach.

"Don't know what to say here, brother," Cam started after another few minutes. "There's no need to do the best man thing and ask if this is what you really want. Know that. Also know it's the right decision for you."

Jamie smiled, tilting his bottle toward Cam. "Congrats, then?"

"Congrats," Cam said, clinking their bottle necks. "Proud of you, Jameson."

"For bagging a hot-as-hell Irishman?"

Cam waggled his eyebrows. "You could've had me for that."

Jamie's own brows raced north, and Cam snorted, expecting that reaction. Even though Cam was bi, and even though Jamie was one of the most handsome men Cam knew, their relationship had never been sexual. Jamie had been his brother from day one.

"Yeah, no," Cam said. "You're totally not my type."

"Too handsome?" Jamie waved a hand around his face like the fucking model he could have been.

"Save that"—Cam mimicked the gesture—"for your husband. As for me, you're way too fucking sweet."

Jamie picked up the stress ball and tossed it at his face. Cam swatted it away, laughing.

Cam couldn't help but be happy for his best friend, who

was grinning like a fool. A lot, these days. "You fought for what you wanted, for who you love, *and* you had the patience to hang on. Don't know if I could have done the same."

Jamie's gaze snuck up the beach again. "You love someone as much as I love Aidan, you'll do anything to hold on to that. He was worth it, all of it."

Cam kicked his shin under the table, damn mooning fool. "Even missing the Final Four?" he teased. It had been their annual ritual, Jamie a two-time national champion who'd always gotten them the good seats. But this year, Aidan and Jamie would still be on their honeymoon during the Big Dance.

"I am sorry about that." Jamie looked genuinely contrite —that too-sweet thing again—and Cam regretted the teasing.

"San Antonio versus a honeymoon in Dublin. Don't blame you one bit," Cam said, letting him off the hook. "Though I am disappointed you didn't get the Gaels into the Tourney."

"Next year," Jamie said, determination lighting his bright blue eyes.

Cam tilted his bottle for another tap. "Will hold you to that."

"You should go. Get out of here for a bit. You've been working nonstop since you moved out."

"The work keeps me distracted."

Jamie's eyes narrowed. "From?"

He should have let the fool moon. Instead, he had triggered those latent investigative tendencies. Cam took a swallow, then mumbled, "Just adjusting."

"Everything good with the house?"

The same words from Nic's text earlier brought the prosecutor to mind again. Jamie was asking about a different house, the one Cam rented from Aidan, but both touched on the same nerve—how out of place he felt here.

"Other than getting the neighbor kid's mail and learning he's got an American Express Black Card and a six-figure job." Jamie whistled low, and Cam nodded. "Twenty-five, fresh out of business school, and just bought a million-and-a-half-dollar cottage."

"I hate to tell you," Jamie said, "but the sticker shock never wears off."

Cam hung his head, picking at the label on his bottle. "Fuck me."

"You know, if you ever—"

Beer lurched in Cam's gut. "I'll manage," he said, silencing the offer from Jamie he never wanted to hear. He wasn't that desperate yet. "Aidan's cutting me a screaming deal on the rent. That's hard enough to swallow."

"You're my best friend, and like I said, you transferring to the field office out here means I can do my dream job *and* sleep at night."

"Next to your hot-as-hell Irishman?" Cam said with a smirk, deflecting.

"Especially that." Jamie laughed, and the heavy mood lifted. "You're family, Cam, and you know we take care of family."

"Like I took care of your grumpy ass through rehab and nerd school?"

Several years Jamie had been in his neck of the woods, getting his crypto grad degree at MIT after an injury ended his NBA career. Before he'd joined the FBI.

"Exactly like that." Jamie reached a hand across the

table, laying it over his. "I couldn't have asked for a better brother."

Jamie's grin, his sincerity, and his blasted sweetness were infectious. Cam let the potent combination wash over him, let it wash away his worries, at least for this weekend. "Me too, Whiskey," he said, smiling. "And I couldn't be prouder to stand next to you tomorrow."

MEL

"Three glasses of Stagg, neat, and"—the bartender placed a salt-rimmed highball on the tray with the whiskeys—"La Paloma."

Mel signed the bill and closed the billfold, passing it back across the bar. "Much obliged," she said with a smile, already anticipating the salt, grapefruit, and tequila hitting her tongue.

"You need a refill, just ring up." The twenty-something bartender threw her a wink. "I'm at your service."

Mel appreciated the attention, especially from a handsome fellow half her age. She flashed her canary diamond ring all the same, happily married as she was.

"Lucky guy," the bartender said.

"Lucky me," she returned, smiling.

She picked up the tray of drinks, balancing it on one hand, a skill she'd perfected as a waitress in her dad's restaurants, and headed downstairs to the hotel spa. She pushed open the French doors and followed the sounds of voices through the darkened lobby to the lit-up nail lounge in the back. The spa was primarily for facials, massages, and the like, but blowouts and nails were popular with the wedding crowd. Of which they were a part this weekend.

Her husband, half perched on one of the vanities, lifted a cheek for a kiss. Mel gave it to him as she slid the tray onto the gleaming marble next to him. Danny blindly reached for a whiskey, eyes tracking a pacing Aidan. "You sure you want to do this, big bro?" Mel was surprised Danny was questioning Aidan. Then again, no one wanted to deal with Aidan on the warpath after a decision he regretted.

A vanity over, friend and stylist Cory grumbled, "I did not haul my ass all the way out here to this fancy-pants hotel for nothing."

"A whiskey for your trouble." Mel set a glass out of the way of the red-hued dyes Cory was mixing in a bowl.

"If he—" Danny started, only to be cut off by the groom himself.

"I want to." Aidan grabbed the last whiskey off the tray and plopped into the salon chair.

"Semipermanent again?" Cory asked.

Last year, Aidan had dyed his hair red, his natural color, for an undercover gig, but it had only been temporary, both the cover and his hair.

Aidan took a bigger-than-he-should gulp of fifty-dollar-a-glass sipping whiskey. "No, permanent dye this time."

Danny whistled. "Jamie's going to lose his shit."

"That's the point," Aidan said with a wink, some of his confidence restored. "Besides, what else am I supposed to get him for a wedding gift?"

Mel sank into the other chair, crossing one leg over the other as she enjoyed the first citrusy sip of her cocktail. She lowered the glass and tapped a nail against her lips. "Let's see . . . Maybe you could get him more than a couple months off the almost-killed-again roller coaster?"

Danny choked on his drink, and Aidan shot her a teasing glare. "You're one to talk."

"At least you're behind a desk now."

"Didn't stop you from doing fieldwork on occasion."

She shrugged one shoulder. "I didn't have a husband at home."

"Hey!" Danny squawked, nudging her arm with his dangling foot.

"*Then,*" she added with a smile.

"Hasn't stopped you now either. Not that I'd want you to." Danny traded the vanity for the arm of her chair. "I rather like being married to a certified badass."

Her turn to lift a cheek for a kiss, and the thread between their hearts thrummed as light filled her from the inside out. She still didn't know how she'd been lucky enough to find a partner who understood her so well, who loved her so well, and who never tried to put her in a cage. In her best friend's little brother, no less. Danny let her be who she was, in all respects—made her better in all those same respects—so she tried not to give him too hard a time when the Don Juan side of her husband came out to play. As long as it was with her. And on the occasion they shared, it was together, on terms they agreed. Truth be told, she had come to love the fun, flirty Danny as much as she loved the responsible one who ran the family company and the dedicated one who would do anything for their friends and family, including risking his own neck.

Jamie understood all that about Aidan too; the Talley boys were more than a little similar despite their ten-year age gap. She laid a hand on her husband's thigh as she smiled at Aidan. "I doubt Jamie expects you to live behind the desk either."

"No, he doesn't. He understands too." Aidan shared her smile, happy and content, before he flapped a hand at his dyed blond locks. "But I ain't dying this shit again," he added, the Southern tell he'd picked up from Jamie doubly hilarious with his Irish lilt. "Other than to keep the gray out, so no more undercover gigs."

Cory stepped between the chairs, bowl and brush in hand. "You keep going on TV with your future husband after ball games, and everyone will know who you are anyways, no matter your hair color."

"He's right," Danny said. "No one likes a camera hog."

Mel swatted his leg, but in good humor, all of them laughing.

"Cut it too?" Cory asked, running a comb through Aidan's longer than usual strands.

"Just a trim. Leave it long." A devilish smirk spread across his face.

Mel knew that look, something else the Talley boys shared, though Mel didn't want to know anything about it on the elder one's face.

"Seriously, though," she said after another swallow of her drink. "How are you handling the SAC's chair?"

"It's fine. You trained me well." He polished off his whiskey and started to lean forward, only to have Cory jerk him back.

"We gonna go through this shit again?" Cory said, scissors and comb held aloft, a near miss at an ill-timed whack.

"I've got cuffs if need be," Mel said with a wink.

Sputtering, Danny leaned forward and took the glass

from Aidan, who seemed as desperate to move on from her remark as she had been from his earlier one. "It helps having a friend in the US Attorney's Office," he said.

"You and Price might actually be able to rein in Bowers." If she was a certified badass, Nic's boss, US Attorney Bowers, was a certified asshole.

"That's the plan. And to try to stay out of the line of fire."

That was saying something for Aidan. "Good," Danny said. "We'll all sleep better at night."

Cory set aside the scissors, trim done, and Aidan gritted his teeth at the first touch of the dye brush. From either the sting, the cold, or just saying goodbye to the blond locks once and for all, returning to his original red, Mel didn't know. She didn't stifle her laugh either.

"What about you two?" Cory asked, glancing over Aidan's head to her and Danny. "After that Christmas fiasco?"

"The almost-exploding ship," Danny said, "had nothing on my mother when she found out we'd eloped."

Mel guzzled the tequila-heavy bottom of her cocktail, then set the glass aside. "Hopefully me marrying off her other son tomorrow stems that tide."

Aidan started forward again but caught himself before Cory had to chide him. "Mel, are you sure—"

"I already had this conversation with him," she said, jutting a thumb at Danny.

"But Gabe . . ."

There was a touch of sadness in the corner of her heart her brother would always hold, but the rest of it was so full these days she could bear it. Her brother would want her to be happy, and he would want the same for the man he had ultimately given his life for. "Gabe would be ecstatic that you found a good man to love again. He'd want you to be happy."

"You think?" Aidan asked, voice hoarse.

"I mean, he'd rib you for being a ball bunny, but you have a type." Hilarity erupted on all sides, and Danny dropped another kiss on her head. When their amusement subsided, she reached out a hand, grasping Aidan's forearm. "I actually love that he's a part of the wedding tomorrow, through me."

Aidan covered her hand with his, squeezing. "So do I."

AIDAN

Aidan clipped in his clover cuff links, adjusted his matching emerald ascot, and shrugged into his morning jacket, flipping out the tails. Checking himself in the mirror, he was startled by the man staring back at him.

A man on his wedding day.

He'd never thought he would get another one. When his first husband had died, Aidan believed his shot at true love was gone. Because Gabe had been that, no question. His true love, the love of his life. Aidan missed him every day still, and he'd made sure to include Gabe in this day, from the anniversary cuff links on his wrists to Mel officiating the ceremony. He would always love Gabe, and that love was in no way diminished by the truths Aidan had learned last year or by the fact Aidan had found love again. Gabe wasn't the *only* love of his life. What he had with Jamie was true love too, the second love of his life.

An Irishman through and through, having lucked out in love, twice.

And he was getting married this second time on St. Patrick's Day.

In some ways, Aidan felt and looked more like himself today than he had on his first wedding day. Jamie drew that out of him, from the red hair to the dancing eyes to being in the best shape of his life in his midforties. The younger man kept him on his toes—in the office when Jamie consulted, on the court when Aidan played ball with him, and at home in their bed. But it was more than his physical appearance that struck Aidan. Despite the added stress of the SAC job, he felt settled. In his work, in his heart, and in his home. Jamie had been right when he'd said married life looked good on him. They had already been living as such for eight months. Aidan couldn't wait to make it official.

A knock on the door came right on time, saving him from bouncing on his toes like an excited kid. "Coming!" He checked his appearance one last time, pocketed his wallet, and was silencing his phone as he opened the door.

Then immediately tried to slam it closed. "What the hell are you doing, Whiskey?" He struggled against his fiancé, who had thrust an arm between the door and jamb, trying to shoulder his way inside. "This is bad luck."

"There's no bride in there," Jamie said, using his height and heft to overpower Aidan's resistance. Two steps inside he froze, baby blues growing round as saucers. "I only see a groom, who's a redhead again."

Aidan closed the door, hand lingering on the knob. "I wanted to surprise you. You like it?"

Big, warm hands closed over his shoulders and Jamie turned him around, backing him up against the door. "Do you even need to ask that, Irish?"

His gaze flickered up to Jamie's freshly shaven face. Full

lips curved in a wide, easy smile, high cheekbones lightly pinked, the brightest blue eyes Aidan had ever seen. Fuck, he was gorgeous, worthy of every camera that had ever turned its lens on him, and he was looking at Aidan like he'd hung the moon.

"I couldn't think what else to get you as a wedding present," Aidan said.

Jamie cupped his face, thumb brushing over his cheek. "You didn't have to get me anything except you."

"You've given me everything." He angled his face into Jamie's hand, kissing his palm. "It was the least I could do. And I wanted to do it for me too."

Hand diving into his hair, Jamie tilted his head back and kissed his neck, just above the stiff shirt collar. "Can I show you how much I appreciate it?"

Aidan gasped, clutching Jamie's biceps with one hand and the back of his head with the other, intending to pull him off, but Jamie's lips and tongue were doing marvelous things to him. "Whiskey . . ."

Jamie stepped closer, grinding that big body up against his. "Let me show you, baby."

He wanted the show, all of it, but not when they might be interrupted before they reached the climax. "If it involves my cock in your mouth, it'll have to wait." He hauled Jamie's flushed face out of his neck. "We're due downstairs in ten, and our mothers will kill us if we show up with come-stained tuxes."

"I can be neat."

Aidan laughed out loud. "Since when?"

"Since today."

Aidan lowered a hand and palmed Jamie through his

dress pants. "I don't believe you," he whispered hotly in his ear. "And I don't want to be neat tonight."

Jamie thrust against him, groaning. "Fuck, Irish."

"I mean to, baby."

Another louder moan.

Aidan nipped his earlobe. A step too far, apparently. Taking hold of his shoulders, Jamie slammed him back against the door and attacked his mouth with the same need building in Aidan. It was always there, a low-level simmer for the man he loved, but after a night apart, simmer was well on its way to boiling, heat stoked by Jamie's tongue down his throat and hands on his ass. Whoever thought keeping them apart last night was a good idea was going to have to answer to their mothers, because at the rate they were going . . .

Banging on the door rattled Aidan's spine. "Brothers!" Danny shouted. "Stop making out and let's go."

Jamie rested his head on Aidan's shoulder. "How does he know?"

"Because I could hear you moaning through the door," Danny replied.

Chuckling, Aidan kissed Jamie's cheek, then very reluctantly pushed him away and shoved off the door. He helped set his fiancé to rights—hair, jacket, and ascot—and Jamie did the same for him.

"You look beautiful," Aidan whispered with one last tweak of Jamie's collar.

"So do you." Jamie's hand lingered at his temple, the gentle touch sending shivers down Aidan's spine. "And I'll show you how much I appreciate *this* tonight."

"Holding you to that." He clasped Jamie's hand and opened the door to a grinning Danny.

"You two done?" his brother asked.

"For now."

Two doors down they snagged Cam, who, despite his scowl, was the picture of elegance in a morning suit, his big, bruiser frame filling it out nicely.

Until he opened his mouth.

"Where the fuck did you go?" he said to Jamie.

The sounded like *da*, and *fuck* had a clipped harshness to it only a true Southie could pull off.

Aidan struggled not to laugh. "To make out with me," he barely managed.

Cam shook a finger at him. "That's bad luck and you know it." The Boston tirade continued down the elevator and out the French doors to the event lawn. Rounding the corner, they came upon what Aidan had long considered one of the best views of the California coast. Situated high atop an ocean bluff, the Ritz was surrounded on three sides by pristine golf greens and on the other by the Pacific Ocean. Today, the picture-perfect bluff was set with rows of green-ribboned white chairs, an aisle between them leading to a flowering arbor, and, everywhere Aidan looked, their friends and family.

Two of whom—a pair of lanky brunette twins—were careening right for them. Jamie's nieces crashed into their uncle and Jamie laughed, the sound bright and carefree, music to Aidan's ears. "We're supposed to take you to Grandma," one of them said. "You too," the other one said to Cam. They'd each grabbed a hand and were already tugging the pair forward.

"Duty calls," Jamie said. "I'll meet you at the front."

"Count on it," Aidan replied.

"And my wife calls," Danny added, nodding to where Mel stood beneath the arbor, crooking a finger at him.

"Go," Aidan said. "She's the last person we want to piss off today."

"Seems a wise idea," Danny replied with a wink. "And looks like you won't be lonely long." He pointed at the strawberry blond child on their sister's hip, wriggling herself free.

Dressed in a poufy green and white dress, Katie hit the ground running. Aidan knelt and braced for impact, the little girl charging him full speed.

"Uncle Ai!" She flung herself into his arms, giggling. They hugged each other tight before she pulled back and thrust her wrist under his nose. Tied to it was a small silk pillow and to it, two titanium rings, one inlaid with emeralds, the other with aquamarines. "I get to carry flowers *and* rings."

"I know." He righted the pillow on her wrist. "I wouldn't have it any other way." Katie was his niece, one of seven niblings, but she was also his and Gabe's goddaughter, another way his late husband was a part of today's celebration.

"She's been showing those off to everyone," came a voice above them.

Aidan glanced up, more than a little surprised to see Nic standing there. It had been a fifty-fifty shot whether Nic would show—past awkwardness getting in the way of current friendship—but Nic was that, a friend, and a valuable coworker and team member whom Aidan and Jamie had wanted here today. Aidan was happy he had come and happy he didn't look too tired, especially since he'd been covering their case last night.

"No date?" Aidan teased.

Nic's blue eyes, the same color as the tie he wore with an attractive light gray suit, danced as he bent down next to Katie. "Will you be my date?"

"Nic-Nic!" she shouted, her nickname for him since last spring. She threw her arms around his neck, bonking the back of his head with the heavy rings. Just as quickly, she unwound herself and ran screaming up the aisle, bragging, "Nic-Nic's my date!"

"Now you've gone and done it," Aidan said as he and Nic stood. "Ruined her for guys her own age."

"I couldn't exactly show up to this shindig stag." He gestured at Aidan's hair. "And you showing up red? Just for today, or are you leaving it this time?"

Aidan's eyes strayed to his soon-to-be husband. "For good."

"Well, it looks good," Nic said with a smile. "And so do you."

"Thank you for coming," Aidan said, then nodded at the bar. "And for supplying the beer."

"No problem. Couldn't have Boston spitting out your fancy champagne."

They were still laughing when Danny sidled up next to him. "There's an angry bounty hunter up front demanding we get started." Aidan glanced past him to where Mel stood tapping her designer heel next to Jamie and Cam.

"Who decided to make the deadliest woman alive the officiant?" Nic added.

"Oh, that would be me," Danny said, raising a hand. "Because even the deadliest woman alive is afraid of my mother. Now, best not keep my wife waiting. She can get feisty." His smile stretched into a telling leer.

Aidan winced. "We've had this talk, baby bro. Don't want to hear it."

Danny strutted away cackling, Aidan following, until he realized Nic wasn't with them. He turned back to find Nic stalled out by the last row of chairs.

"I'll just sit here," Nic said.

Aidan waved him forward. "You'll sit with the family, Dominic."

The prosecutor seemed at a loss for words, a rare sight on a rare day indeed.

"You are Katie's date, aren't you?" Aidan added, offering him an out.

Nic took it, clearing his throat and buttoning his suit coat as he strode forward. "That I am."

Aidan waited for him to slide into the open aisle seat next to Katie's mother before he turned forward, looking ahead to Jamie and his future. Gazes locked, heart tearing at his chest, Aidan took the last few steps to the arbor where the love of the rest of his life waited. He'd have run if he wouldn't have looked like a fool.

"You two ready?" Mel asked as Aidan twined his hand with Jamie's.

Aidan turned to face his partner. "You ready to make this partnership forever, Whiskey?"

Jamie lifted his hand, kissing their knuckles. "I'm ready, Irish."

NIC

Vows and rings exchanged, the terrace room doors were thrown open, and wedding guests migrated between the tables and food inside to the bar and dancing outside. Down a few steps from the main lawn, Nic stood by one of the fire pits, nursing a bottle of his brewery's Imperial Stout. He watched Cam, jacket and ascot long gone, dance with Nic's "date," Katie wobbling on top of the ASAC's feet. During the ceremony, she had run to Nic after her ring-bearing duties were done, but once the dancing started, and he'd told her he didn't dance, she'd abandoned him for her "other uncles." Cam had pulled out all his Mr. Potato Head faces, interacting with her as naturally as he did with adults, not a care in the world if Katie's icing-covered fingers marred his suit pants or if her shoes scuffed his Oxfords.

At forty-five, Nic could tear apart a witness in court or have them eating out of his hand, depending on which he needed for his case, but around kids he was clueless. Katie had been the first to bully past his awkwardness and force him to like her. At the moment, though, he felt a little green toward the giggling tyke. She was dancing with the man Nic would admit only to himself that he'd wanted for a while now. To the point he had shuttered the rest of his dalliances, Aidan the last man he'd dated over a year ago. But Nic hadn't made a move on Cam yet either, even if his gut burned every time he saw Cam flirting with another person. Getting involved with the ASAC of the Bureau office his US Attorney's Office worked with daily wasn't smart.

A waft of tequila on the sea breeze cut through the smell of beer and smoke, as did the *click-clack* of heels over the crackling fire. Glancing left, Nic spotted Mel, in her long green gown and death-defying heels, descending the stairs on the other side of the firepit. "We missed you at the rehearsal dinner," she said, circling to stand next to him.

Had they really? Or would his presence have made everything awkward, like he'd felt most of today? He also hadn't lied about being busy with work. "I heard the food was excellent," he said, then took another swig. "Sorry I missed it."

"Thank you," Mel replied, to his confusion, before clarifying, "for covering the case you're working with Aidan so he could enjoy this weekend."

Of course she knew. The woman had been out of the Bureau almost a year now, but Nic suspected she was more connected than ever, officially and otherwise.

"You didn't want a big party like this?" Nic asked, deflecting.

"Everyone keeps asking me that, and the answer is still

no. You think I'd want to deal with *that* twice?" She tilted her glass toward the piano Danny and Cam had commandeered—one playing the high notes, the other low—with stout-and-whiskey-fueled gusto. "World of no."

Nic almost lost his drink, spluttering around a gulp of beer. "Point taken."

"I just hope today smooths things over with Danny's mother. Not sure she'll ever forgive me for eloping with her baby."

The Talley matriarch stood across the lawn with Jamie and Aidan, fingering her son's red hair, now closer to her own gray-streaked auburn.

Nic had heard talk of how Aidan had once reverted from his usual dyed blond to his natural red for an undercover case, but Nic hadn't seen the red until today. The change was startling and attractive. As was the smile splitting Aidan's face, which didn't falter as he looked up and spotted him and Mel.

The smile on the face of the other groom beside him seemed to though, just a bit, reminding Nic again that maybe he shouldn't be here. Granted, he and Aidan had never fucked, but that detail hadn't mattered much to Jamie, who at the time had been battling Aidan for more than casual. Jamie had obviously won, blowing through Aidan's defenses, and the past was supposedly behind them all, enough life-and-death close calls over the past year to wipe the slate clean.

Supposedly.

For Mel, though, Nic figured today put her firmly in the clear. "I think she's forgiven you." Nic tilted his beer bottle, and Mel clinked her glass against it.

"Hey, no toasting without us!" Cam jumped over the ledge on the other side of the firepit, skipping the stairs altogether. "And why the fuck is the beer not green? It's fucking St. Patrick's Day."

The comment, in Cam's whiskey-soaked accent, should have been amusing, but it landed like a punch to Nic's gut. "Boston, you ever do that to perfectly good beer, *my* beer, and you're dead to me."

"I'm guessing Mr. Beer Snob didn't bring any cans then either?"

"No," Nic answered straight-faced, for about a second, until Cam's surly expression almost made him lose his drink again. "I did, however, bring some empty metal growlers."

"Fuck yeah," Danny said as he jumped over the ledge behind Cam. "Together with the soda cans and Oreo wrappers I collected last night, we can make a right mess of this." He rubbed his hands together with devilish glee. "I think we're set for our date with a certain lady."

"Are you two sure about this?" Mel asked. "That car is their baby."

Cam tossed a set of keys in the air. "No permanent damage, I swear."

Mel turned to Nic, brow raised. "Should we supervise?"

"I think that would be wise. And I think we're gonna need refills."

He was at the bar, getting another round of beers and a cocktail for Mel, when the groom he least expected appeared at his side.

"Walker," Nic greeted.

"Meant to thank you earlier for the beach house and the beer," Jamie said. "Both were big hits."

"Glad to hear it."

"Also wanted to thank you for coming today." Jamie cleared his throat. "And for helping make all this possible."

Nic couldn't find the words, surprised into silence for the second time today. Jamie's olive branch made little sense, especially after the seeming falter in his earlier smile. Or maybe he'd only imagined that. "I don't—"

"Last spring could have gone very differently. You played a big part in making it go the right way, rescuing Aidan and Katie and getting us all cleared." He held out his hand. "I owe you for that, Price. Thank you."

"You're welcome," Nic said, shaking it, and hoping he didn't sound as off-kilter as he felt, this whole day like someone else's life. Certainly not his. "Try and make sure Aidan relaxes some on the honeymoon?"

"You help hold down the fort here, and I'll see what I can do."

"It's a deal."

The bartender set a Paloma next to the beers, and Jamie warily eyed the drinks. "Try and make sure they don't ruin the Chevelle too."

"Your best friend thinks the beer should be green. He's not giving me a lot to work with."

Jamie rolled his eyes. "Rag him about the Patriots," he said, mischief dancing in his gaze. "That'll make him forget all about the green beer. And hopefully also about ruining our car."

"That sounds like fun," Nic said, likewise feeling up to some mischief. "Give us twenty minutes?"

With a nod, Jamie wandered back to his new husband, and Nic grabbed the three beer bottles by their necks and the Paloma in his other hand. He followed the cobblestone path around to the front of the hotel where Danny and Cam had annexed one corner of the valet area, the former tying growlers, wrappers, and soda cans to the back of the Chevelle, while the latter shook a spray can of whipped cream. For her part, Mel sat perched on the fountain ledge, bouncing one knee over the other as she monitored the children. Nic handed the Paloma to her first, then took the beers over to the guys.

"I have a question," he said, standing next to Cam near the hood of the car. "Who's the better quarterback, Montana or Brady?"

Cam whipped his head around so fast they almost bumped noses. "You really wanna have this argument with me?"

"I asked the question, didn't I?"

"Brady. No question."

"Oh, that's my cue!" Danny straightened from tying on the last growler. "Definitely Montana."

The argument roped in even Mel, who, as a Miami native, lobbied hard for Marino. It was enough to keep the troublemakers outside the car and limited the whipped cream shenanigans to IRISH & WHISKEY on the hood and JUST MARRIED on the back windshield.

"Well played," Mel whispered to Nic as they stood on the edge of the wedding crowd twenty minutes later.

Clover and rainbow confetti showered the grooms as they hustled out, and Jamie mouthed a *Thank you* over his shoulder at Nic. Cam tossed the beach house keys through the window, and Jamie revved the engine, peeling away to raucous applause.

Crowd dispersing, Danny held an arm out to Mel. "Another dance, wife?"

She looped her elbow through his. "Twist my arm, husband." They joined the group of guests headed back to the lawn, Cam with them.

Nic, unfortunately—or maybe not, as he'd had enough socializing for one day—needed to check in on his case. He was waiting at the elevators when a shout of "Dominic!" rang out behind him.

Cam stalked across the lobby toward him, visibly perturbed that Nic had tried to duck out early. "I'm not done arguing with you." Or maybe he just wanted to go another few rounds. "Let's talk Super Bowls. Number of appearances?"

Nic played along for the chance to get the last word. And he was going to get it. He'd saved his ace in the hole, anticipating Cam wouldn't let this drop. Arguing was what they did best, after all. "Four," he answered.

"Eight for Brady. Super Bowl MVPs?"

"Three," Nic answered as Cam stepped past him into the elevator.

"Four." Cam hit the button for his floor, then Nic his. "Super Bowl wins?"

"Four." Nic bit the inside of his cheek, holding back the question he wanted to ask so badly.

"Five," Cam shot back. "Brady's got him beat, hands down."

"Okay, Boston, here's one for you . . . How many times did Montana *lose* a Super Bowl?"

Oh, how those lovely dark eyes blazed.

"I'm sorry." Nic held a hand up to his ear. "I didn't hear your answer."

"None," Cam gritted out between clenched teeth.

"Right, none," Nic said. "And Brady lost to who? Oh,

that's right, twice to Eli fucking Manning and once to a fucking backup." Nic planed his arms like a flying bird and grinned. "Fly, Eagles fly." Cam's face reddened, the color in his cheeks even lovelier than his swirling black eyes. "Is that the Manning Face you're—"

The rest of Nic's words died, silenced by a whiskey-and-stout-laced kiss. Cam had flown across the cab, grabbed his chin, and shut him up faster than a judge's gavel. The taste of his beer on Cam's lips, on his tongue, was enough to blank Nic's mind, to make him groan his want down the agent's throat. Taking advantage, Cam shoved him back against the elevator wall and dove deeper into the kiss.

But Nic didn't let him hold the upper hand for long. He wanted a deeper taste too. Hands tunneling through Cam's dark hair, he forced his tongue between Cam's lips and claimed a better taste of the mouth he'd wanted for months. And fuck him if it wasn't better than his wildest dreams. Just like the hard body pressed against him and the other hard parts grinding against each other. If Nic kept going, there was only one place this would lead. Where his dreams always did these past months. But those dreams were just that, fantasies. Because reality, making itself known again with the ding of the elevator, stood between them.

Cam saved him the wasted willpower, pulling back first for breath, Nic's jaw still held in his hand. "If you ever accuse me of having Manning Face again, I swear I will turn a keg of your best beer green."

"I believe this is your floor, Agent Byrne." Using one of the moves he'd learned as a Navy SEAL, Nic easily dislodged Cam's hold, got behind him, and shoved him out of the elevator. But not before copping a feel of Cam's firm, round ass. "Later, Boston."

Cam grinned over his shoulder, dark eyes heavy-lidded. "Sooner, Price."

Against his better judgment, Nic sure the hell hoped so.

JAMIE

Standing by the beach house bay window, Jamie ignored the ocean view in favor of the titanium and emerald circle around his left ring finger. A part of Aidan to carry with him every day.

Partners, always.

That was what they had promised a year ago and reaffirmed today, in vows written by their niece. Jamie smiled, remembering the perfect simplicity of Katie's words.

I, Uncle Jamie, take you, Uncle Ai, to be my husband.

To make you smile big and make you happy forever.

I love you, and that seals the promise.

Jamie had added *Partners, always,* as he'd slipped his ring on Aidan's finger, voicing the promise he was making, swearing before God, the law, and all their gathered friends and family.

Autumn eyes glassy, Aidan had repeated the same vows back to him, added the same promise as he'd slid the ring on Jamie's finger, and a watery laugh had escaped at the end when Katie giggled and clapped with glee.

Mel had pronounced them husbands, and they'd kissed, longer than was strictly polite, to boisterous applause.

So much happiness. Jamie didn't know what to do with it all. His chest felt as if it would explode, too much love and joy trying to cram in there. When he'd left the NBA a decade ago, he'd never dreamed he would wind up here. Coaching the sport he loved, making a difference in kids' lives. Out of the closet and showing off his fiancé—now husband—every chance he got. Having the love of two families who accepted him, of friends who would risk their lives for him, and of a brilliant, gorgeous man who had conquered demons, real and emotional, to love him.

To marry him.

His own eyes grew damp, the emeralds refracting like a prism.

He blinked the wetness back as strong arms circled him from behind. "You've been quiet since we left the reception," Aidan said, propping his chin on his shoulder.

The contentment in his husband's lightly accented voice, the Irish lilt escaping more freely, almost brought the tears back. As it was, Jamie struggled to force out words around the lump in his throat. "I'm happy."

"Me too." Aidan tangled his left hand with his, their rings clinking together. Emerald green and Carolina blue, side by side. Danny had lobbied for whiskey-colored topaz, but Aidan had demanded the blue, to match Jamie's eyes. Jamie would have been fine with either, his ring on Aidan's finger all he needed. "Thank you, Whiskey, for marrying me today."

Jamie's chuckle sounded as waterlogged as Aidan's laugh during the wedding. "Hardly a trouble."

"But I was, and I'm sorry for that trouble, for ever

hurting you." Using the hand in his, Aidan turned him around and cupped his cheek with the other. "You scared the hell out of me, Jameson Walker."

Jamie lifted a hand, lightly holding Aidan's wrist. "Scared you?"

"The prospect of loving you, of having this, then losing it, terrified me." Aidan leaned forward, softly kissing his lips. "I didn't make this easy on you. I hid behind my grief, my job, other . . . walls, but you chipped away at them."

Jamie returned the gentle kiss, banishing thoughts of those first few confusing months of their relationship, the rough parts, at least. The good parts he cherished still. Sex on every surface of his—now their—home. Seeing Aidan with the red hair back. Learning from one of the best agents in the Bureau. Those parts, and the love for this man that had sunk its claws in deep, had kept him hanging on. "I'm persistent when I know what I want."

Aidan chuckled. "More like a fucking bulldozer." The next kiss lingered, ramping up the need stirring in Jamie as they pushed each other's morning jackets off. "Thank you for not giving up on me."

The emeralds of Aidan's cuff links reminded Jamie he was grateful too. He'd also hidden behind secrets that could have torn them apart forever. "Thank you for forgiving me."

Aidan shook his head. "Nothing to apologize for, baby."

God, Jamie loved hearing Aidan utter that endearment, his Irish burr making it sexy as hell. He closed the distance between them, hands weaving into the auburn locks, tilting Aidan's head to take more than just a kiss. Aidan melted against him, body warm and eager.

Mouth sliding off his, Aidan nibbled down his jaw as he

worked Jamie's ascot free. "How about we move on to the wedding night portion of the festivities?"

Jamie liked that plan until Aidan got to the buttons of his tuxedo vest, and he recalled what he'd stashed in the ivory pocket there. "Irish, wait."

"Tired of waiting, especially after that prewedding stunt of yours." Aidan nosed aside his collar and sucked what would surely be a bruise into the crook of his neck. "You were so eager to get your mouth around my cock earlier."

"Five minutes," Jamie bargained, pushing Aidan away and holding him back with two hands. "I promise it'll be worth it." One look at those smoldering autumn eyes and Jamie debated his own promise, but then Aidan's hand, traveling south, smoothed over Jamie's vest pocket and halted.

"Is that a flash drive in your pocket, Walker?"

Jamie fished out the plastic device. "Seemed appropriate." He grinned sheepishly, holding it out to Aidan. "Your wedding present."

"There's something good on it, I hope?"

He grabbed Aidan's other hand and led him into the kitchen where he had a laptop open. "See for yourself."

Aidan hesitated, eyes bouncing from him to the flash drive to the computer.

"It won't bite," Jamie said, circling behind him. He draped his arms over his husband's hips, holding him lightly.

"If it does, I bite you," Aidan said, grin wicked, before he inserted the drive. He clicked open the file directory, and Jamie hid his smile in Aidan's shoulder. He'd named the file "FBIGuy74." Aidan's less-than-original gamer tag had been a frequent source of amusement, to Jamie, at least.

Aidan kicked his shin. "Think you're funny, don't you?"

"Fucking hilarious." Jamie kissed Aidan's temple while they waited.

Aidan startled when *Destiny* loaded on the screen, then startled again when his characters appeared, all of them at max level. "What did you do?"

"Go check your vault."

He clicked his Hunter first, viewing her gear. "Holy shit. This is all the best stuff? How—"

"Might have robbed Xur."

Aidan ran through the same checks on his Titan and Warlock, cackling with glee. "You hacked the game, you big, beautiful genius." Aidan's grin was huge, splitting his handsome face in two. "When did you do this?"

"While I was on the road with the team, since I know you haven't had time to play lately, with work and the wedding. It's not much . . ."

Aidan shifted, hip against the counter, angling toward him. "Neither is a little hair dye, but it's who we are, isn't it?"

"Yeah, it is." Jamie went in for a kiss, only to whiff as Aidan whipped back around to the computer.

"Wait, wait, wait." Aidan hunched over the laptop, blocking Jamie's view of the screen. He straightened after another minute, revealing his new gamer tag.

StickyHeel12DH.

Jamie snickered. "My 'Dear Husband,' huh?"

"This is who I am now." Aidan cupped his cheek again, smile shifting from amused to affectionate. "And you're mine." He gave him a soft peck, then, eyes darkening, shifted so his thigh slipped between Jamie's legs, rubbing against Jamie's hardening erection. "Now about that other present?"

Jamie growled. "Thought you'd never ask."

It was a wonder they didn't take a header down the spiral staircase, mouths attached, legs tangled, hands shedding layers of tuxes step by step. They were naked, save for their wedding bands, by the time they hit the bed. Jamie tumbled back first, Aidan coming down on top of him and giving him only a second to catch his breath before stealing another kiss.

Jamie groaned and rocked his hips, chasing the feel of Aidan hard and slick against him. Helping him out, Aidan reached between them and grasped both of their cocks in his hand, pumping. Everything was hot—Aidan's grip, his cock, his mouth devouring Jamie's—then as Aidan slid slower, he burned a path down Jamie's neck to the interlocking *N* and C tattoo on his chest.

"I changed my mind," Aidan said between bites at the ink and licks at Jamie's teased-to-aching nipple. "Want you in *my* mouth."

Jamie almost shot in Aidan's hand, only his confusion at Aidan inching up instead of down saving him.

"Lube?" Aidan asked.

"Bedside table."

He leaned away and opened the drawer, tossing an "On your knees" over his shoulder. "Like looking up at you," he added, rolling back and lubing up his fingers.

Scrambling up, Jamie had to grasp the base of his dick to stave off his rapidly approaching orgasm.

"Problem, Whiskey?" asked the smirking Irishman, who shifted onto his side before Jamie's spread knees.

"I'll tell you how you can—"

Jamie didn't need to finish.

As if reading his mind, Aidan leaned forward and took Jamie's tip in his mouth, circling his head with his tongue, then torturing him with a slow slide all the way to the root. He reached around with his other hand and performed a similar move, lubed finger circling Jamie's hole, before pushing in, the burn terrible and lovely.

Jamie didn't know which he wanted to fuck more, Aidan's mouth or his fingers.

Tossed around in the waves, like that night on the bathroom floor in Galveston, but on his knees this time, all Jamie could do was hold onto Aidan and ride it out. His left hand tangled in the long red locks, emeralds twinkling in his husband's hair, while his other hand wrapped around Aidan's dick, pumping him in time with Aidan's strokes in his ass. Which escalated as Aidan slipped another finger in, going harder, faster, and encouraging Jamie to do the same.

"Fuck, baby," Jamie panted, and Aidan hummed his approval, hips thrusting his cock into Jamie's grip while Jamie flailed in his. The sum total of the pleasure—hot, wet heat around his dick, the pounding against his prostate, Aidan's hard dick in his hand, and the sight of emeralds in his husband's hair—had Jamie right at the edge. All it took was Aidan glancing up, one look into those dark autumn eyes glazed over with lust, and Jamie came, pitching forward and emptying himself down Aidan's throat.

He was still returning to his senses when Aidan rumbled in his ear, "Gonna fuck my husband now."

Then Jamie's face was in the pillow, the cotton cool on his heated skin, muffling his groans as Aidan hauled him up on his hands and knees, ass in the air, and thrust into him. Worked open already, the slight sting gave way to pleasure right away, Aidan filling him up, keeping him flying in his orgasmic haze. Aidan rode him hard, snapping his hips as he nipped at his shoulder, their hands winding together on the pillow. It wasn't long before Aidan's strokes became erratic, and he spilled warm heat into Jamie with a shattered groan.

Arms and legs giving out, Jamie took them down to the mattress together, more than happy with Aidan's warm, heavy weight on top of him, his husband nuzzling the nape of his neck. "How'd I get so lucky?" Aidan mumbled there.

Jamie laid his cheek on the pillow, peeking over his shoulder. "You're Irish."

"We're both lucky." Aidan slid to his side and rotated Jamie onto his too, drawing him into another gentle, lingering kiss.

"Irish, Southern—same stock," Jamie whispered against his lips.

Drawing back, Aidan ran a hand through Jamie's hair and down the side of his face, eyes warm and content, same as Jamie felt. "Love you, Whiskey."

Jamie grasped his husband's left hand, bringing their clasped fists up between them and kissing the side-by-side rings. "Love you too, Irish."

Always was on their lips when they met again, *partners* in their hearts forever.

Reviews are an invaluable tool when it comes to

spreading the word about great reads. Please consider leaving an honest review for *Blended Whiskey* on your favorite review site.

Thank you for reading!

ACKNOWLEDGMENTS

I hope you enjoyed reading this *Agents Irish and Whiskey* short as much as I enjoyed writing it. It was fun to revisit old friends and get a jump start on new ones! Thank you so much, readers, and especially Lushes, for all the *Agents Irish and Whiskey* love. Special thanks as well to everyone who helped me put together this story—first edition editors Deb and Julia, second edition editor Adam, first edition cover artist Natasha Snow, and second edition cover artist Cate Ashwood.

ALSO BY LAYLA REYNE

For the most up-to-date list of titles and a helpful reading order, please visit www.laylareyne.com.

Agents Irish and Whiskey:

Single Malt

Cask Strength

Barrel Proof

Tequila Sunrise

Blended Whiskey

Trouble Brewing:

Imperial Stout

Craft Brew

Noble Hops

Final Gravity

Fog City:

Prince of Killers

King Slayer

A New Empire

Queen's Ransom

Silent Knight

Perfect Play:

Dead Draw

Bad Bishop

King Hunt

Soul to Find:

Icarus and the Devil

Changing Lanes:

Relay

Medley

Freestyle

Table for Two:

The Last Drop

Blue Plate Special

Over a Barrel

Standalone Titles:

Dine With Me

Variable Onset

Sweater Weather

What We May Be

ABOUT THE AUTHOR

Layla Reyne is the author of *What We May Be* and the *Agents Irish and Whiskey, Fog City,* and *Perfect Play* series. A Carolina Tar Heel who spent fifteen years in California, Layla enjoys weaving her bicoastal experiences into her stories, along with adrenaline-fueled suspense and heart pounding romance.

You can find Layla at laylareyne.com, in her reader group on Facebook—Layla's Lushes, and at the following sites:

BB bookbub.com/authors/layla-reyne
facebook.com/laylareyne
instagram.com/laylareyne
tiktok.com/@laylareyne

www.ingramcontent.com/pod-product-compliance
Lightning Source LLC
Chambersburg PA
CBHW071358200726
48294CB00004B/1210
* 9 7 8 1 9 6 2 0 1 0 0 9 2 *